APOLLONIUS OF RHODES

JASON AND THE ARGONAUTS

TRANSLATED BY E. V. RIEU

PENGUIN BOOKS

PENGUIN BOOKS

Published by the Penguin Group
Penguin Books Ltd, 27 Wrights Lane, London W8 5TZ, England
Penguin Books USA Inc., 375 Hudson Street, New York, New York 10014, USA
Penguin Books Australia Ltd, Ringwood, Victoria, Australia
Penguin Books Canada Ltd, 10 Alcorn Avenue, Toronto, Ontario, Canada M4V 3B2
Penguin Books (NZ) Ltd, 182–190 Wairau Road, Auckland 10, New Zealand

Penguin Books Ltd, Registered Offices: Harmondsworth, Middlesex, England

This selection is from E. V. Rieu's translation of
The Voyage of Argo, published in Penguin Classics 1959 and 1971
This edition published 1995
1 3 5 7 9 10 8 6 4 2

Printed in England by Clays Ltd, St Ives plc

Moved by the god of song, I set out to commemorate the heroes of old who sailed the good ship Argo up the Straits into the Black Sea and between the Cyanean Rocks in quest of the Golden Fleece.

It was King Pelias who sent them out. He had heard an oracle which warned him of a dreadful fate—death through the machinations of the man whom he should see coming from the town with one foot bare. The prophecy was soon confirmed. Jason, fording the Anaurus in a winter spate, lost one of his sandals, which stuck in the bed of the flooded river, but saved the other from the mud and shortly after appeared before the king. He had come for a banquet that Pelias was giving in honour of his father Poseidon and all the other gods, except Pelasgian Here to whom he paid no homage. And no sooner did the king see him than he thought of the oracle and decided to send him on a perilous adventure overseas. He hoped that things might so fall out, either at sea or in outlandish parts, that Jason would never see his home again.

The ship was built by Argus, under Athene's eye. But as poets before me have told that tale, I will content myself by recounting the names and lineage of her noble crew, their long sea voyages, and all they achieved in their wanderings. Muses, inspire my lay.

The name which I put first is that of Orpheus, borne, so the story goes, by Calliope herself to her Thracian lover Oeagrus near the heights of Pimplea. They say that with the music of his voice he enchanted stubborn mountain rocks and rushing streams. And testifying still to the magic of his song, there are wild oaks growing at Zone on the coast of Thrace, which he lured down from Pieria with his lyre, rank upon rank of them, like soldiers on the march. Such was Orpheus, lord of Bistonian Pieria, when Jason son of Aeson, acting on a word from Cheiron, enrolled him as a partner in his venture.

Asterion was quick to join them. Born to Cometes beside the eddying waters of Apidanus, he lived at Peiresiae near Mount Phylleium, where great Apidanus and noble Enipeus meet each other and mingle their far-travelled streams.

Next to them came Polyphemus son of Eilatus from his home in Larissa. In his younger days he had fought in the ranks of the mighty Lapithae when they were at war with the Centaurs. But by now his limbs were heavy with age, though he had not lost the fighting spirit of his youth.

Iphiclus next. He was not left behind in Phylace; for he was Jason's uncle. His sister Alcimede, daughter of Phylacus, was Aeson's wife. The bonds of kinship compelled him to enlist.

Then came Ademtus, King of Pherae, rich in sheep. He was not going to linger in his town below Chalcodon's peak.

Erytus and Echion, sons of Hermes and endowed with all his guile, were quick to leave Alope and their many cornfields. Their kinsman Aethalides came also, adding a third to the pair as they set out. He was borne near the waters of Amphrysus by a daughter of Myrmidon, Eupolemeia of Phthia; but the other two were sons of Antianeira daughter of Menetes.

From wealthy Gyrton came Coronus, Caeneus' son, a man of valour, but no better than his father. For Caeneus, so the bards relate, was destroyed by the Centaurs yet remained alive. Unaided by his noble friends he had routed the enemy, and even when they rallied against him they could not bend his back or kill him. Unbroken and unbowed he sank below the earth, overwhelmed by the massive pines with which they beat him down.

Then came Titaresian Mopsus, whom Leto's son,

Apollo, had trained to excel all others in the art of augury from birds. Also Eurydamas, son of Ctimenus, who lived in Dolopian Ctimene near the lake of Xynia.

Menoetius too was sent from Opus by his father, Actor, to join the chieftains in their voyage.

Eurytion and the valiant Eribotes followed, one the son of Teleon, and one of Irus son of Actor. Illustrious Eribotes was Teleon's son; Eurytion was the son of Irus. And with them was a third, Oïleus, the bravest of the brave and a great man for dashing after the enemy when their ranks were giving way.

From Euboea, Canthus came. Canethus son of Abas sent him—not that he hesitated to enlist. Yet there was to be no home-coming for him, no return to Cerinthus. Fate had decided that he and the great seer Mopsus should wander to the ends of Libya to be destroyed. Which shows that Death can overtake us, however far we go: these two were buried in Libya, which is as far from Colchis as the sun travels in a day.

The next to join were Clytius and Iphitus, Wardens of Oechalia and sons of the cruel Eurytus, to whom the Archer-King Apollo gave his bow, though the gift did him little good when he challenged the great giver to a match.

Next came Telamon and Peleus, sons of Aeacus; but not together and not from the same place. In a mad moment they had killed their brother Phocus, and they

4

had to put a long way between Aegina and themselves. Telamon settled in the island of Salamis, but Peleus parted from him and made himself a home in Phthia.

After them, from Attica, came battle-loving Butes son of the excellent Teleon, and Phalerus of the good ashen spear, whom his father Alcon had allowed to go. Alcon had no other sons to look after him when he was old, yet he despatched that only son of his declining years to make his mark among these men of valour. Meanwhile Theseus, finest of the Attic line, who had gone with Peirithous into the underworld, was kept a prisoner in unseen bonds below the earth at Taenarum. Had this pair been with them, the Argonauts would indeed have had a lighter task.

Next, from the Thespian town of Siphae, came Tiphys son of Hagnias, an expert mariner, who could sense the coming of a swell across the open sea, and learn from sun and star when storms were brewing or a ship might sail. Athene herself, the Lady of Trito, had urged him to join the band of chieftains, who had hoped for this accession to their strength and welcomed his arrival. It was a fitting thing that he should be sent them by the very goddess who had built their ship, which she did with Argus son of Arestor working under her direction. No wonder that *Argo* proved the finest of all ships that ever braved the sea with oars.

After them came Phlias, from Araethyrea, where he

lived in affluence through the good will of his father Dionysus in his home by the springs of Asopus.

From Argos came Talaus and Areius sons of Bias, and also the powerful Leodocus, all of whom Pero daughter of Neleus bore. It was on her account that the Aeolid Melampus suffered great hardships in the farmstead of Iphiclus.

And nobody can say that the mighty and stout-hearted Heracles neglected Jason's call. A rumour of the chieftains' gathering came to his ears when he was on a journey and had just arrived from Arcadia in Lyrceian Argos. It was that time he carried on his back, alive, the boar which fed in the thickets of Lampeia near the great Erymanthian swamp. And no sooner did he hear the news than he dropped the boar, tied up as it was, from his broad shoulders at the entrance to the market at Mycenae, and promptly set out—he did not even ask permission of Eurystheus. Hylas, his noble squire, in the first bloom of youth, went with him to carry his arrows and serve as keeper of the bow.

After him came Nauplius, whose lineage we can trace to King Danaus himself. For his father was Clytoneus son of Naubolus; Naubolus was the son of Lernus; and we know that Lernus was the son of Proetus, himself the son of an earlier Nauplius, who proved to be the finest sailor of his time, offspring as he was of one of Danaus' daughters, the lady Amymone, and her lover the Sea-god.

Of all that lived in Argos, Idmon was the last to come, last because his own bird-lore had told him he would die. And yet he came: he was afraid for his good name at home. This Idmon was not really Abas' son, but one whom Apollo had fathered to take his place among the illustrious Aeolids. The god himself had taught him the prophetic art, how birds should be observed, and how to find omens in burnt-offerings.

And now, from Sparta, Aetolian Lede sent the mighty Polydeuces and Castor, that famous master of the racing horse. She had borne these two in Tyndareus' palace at a single birth. She loved them dearly, but she did not try to keep them back: hers was a spirit worthy of the love of Zeus.

From Arene came the sons of Aphareus, Lynceus and the insolent Idas. Both had the courage that great strength inspires. And in addition Lynceus enjoyed the keenest eyesight in the world, if we may credit the report that it came easy to the man even to see things underground.

Periclymenus son of Neleus set forth also. He was the eldest of the sons King Neleus had in Pylos, and Poseidon had endowed him with enormous strength, together with the power when fighting to assume whatever form he might desire in the stress of battle.

Next, from Arcadia came Amphidamas and Cepheus, two sons of Aleus, who possessed the town of Tegea and the estate of Apheidas. Ancaeus followed them and made a third. He was encouraged to go by his father Lycurgus, an elder brother of the pair, who remained at home himself to look after the ageing Aleus, but parted with this son of his to please his brothers. Ancaeus set out clad in a bearskin from Maenalus and brandishing a huge two-edged axe in his right hand; for his grandfather Aleus had hidden his equipment in a corner of the barn, hoping to the very last to find some way of stopping him.

Augeias also came, whose father was believed to be the Sun. Lord of the Eleans, he enjoyed great wealth. And he wished for nothing better than to see the land of Colchis and Aeetes himself, the king of the Colchians.

Asterius and Amphion, sons of Hyperasius, came from Achaean Pellene, a city founded by their grandfather Pelles on the cliffs of Aegialus.

After them, from Taenarum, came Euphemus, the fastest runner in the world, whom Europa daughter of the mighty Tityos bore to Poseidon. This man could run across the rolling waters of the grey sea without wetting his swift feet. His toes alone sank in as he sped along his watery path.

And there were two more of Poseidon's sons who

came. One was Erginus, hailing from the city of illustrious Miletus; and the other, proud Ancaeus, who came from Samos, the seat of Imbrasian Here. Each of these two could boast his skill in seamanship and war.

Next, bidding farewell to Calydon, came the valiant Meleager son of Oeneus, and Laocoon, a brother of Oeneus, though not by the same mother—his mother was a servant-girl. Oeneus had sent Laocoon, who was no longer young, as guardian of his son; and so it was that Meleager found himself among these bold adventurers when he had scarcely ceased to be a boy. Yet I feel that only one more year of training in his Aetolian home might well have made him the best recruit they had, excepting Heracles. Moreover, he was accompanied on his journey by his maternal uncle, Iphiclus son of Thestius, a good fighter both with the javelin and hand to hand.

At the same time came Palaemonius, who was the son, or rather the reputed son, of Olenian Lernus, his real father having been Hephaestus. This accounted for his being lame. Yet no one could have made light of his manhood and his manly form. Indeed, they won him his place in that noble company and he did Jason credit.

From Phocis came Iphitus, the son of Naubolus, himself the son of Ornytus. This man had once been Jason's host, when Jason went to Pytho to consult the oracle about his voyage. He had entertained him there in his own house.

Next came Zetes and Calaïs, children of the North Wind, whom Oreithyia daughter of Erechtheus had borne to Boreas in the wintry borderland of Thrace. It was from Attica that Thracian Boreas had brought her there. She was whirling in the dance on the banks of Ilissus when he snatched her up and carried her far away to a spot called Sarpedon's Rock, near the flowing waters of Erginus, where he wrapped her in a dark cloud and overcame her. And now, these sons of hers could soar into the sky. Astounding spectacle! As they flapped the wings on either side of their ankles, a glint of gold shone through from spangles on the dusky feathers; and their black locks streaming from head and neck along their backs were tossed by the wind to this side and that.

Last, not even Acastus, son of the great King Pelias himself, had any wish to stay behind in his father's palace. Nor had Argus, who had built the ship under Athene's orders. They too were planning to enlist.

Such and so many were the noblemen who rallied to the aid of Aeson's son. The people of the place called them all Minyae, since most of them and all the best could claim descent from the daughters of Minyas. Thus, Jason himself was the son of Alcimede, whose mother was Clymene, one of Minyas' daughters.

Everything was ready. *Argo* had been equipped by the serfs with all that goes into a well-found ship when business takes people overseas. And now her crew made their way through the city to where she lay on the shore called Magnesian Pagasae. A throng of eager townsfolk gathered round them. But they themselves stood out like bright stars in a cloudy sky; and as the people watched them hurrying along in their armour, one man voiced the thoughts of all.

'Lord Zeus!' he cried. 'What is Pelias doing? Into what exile from Achaea is he banishing this crowd of noblemen? If Aeetes won't give them the fleece of his own free will, they could send his palace up in flames on the very day they land. But they must get there first; and the going will be hard.'

Such was the general feeling in the town. Meanwhile the women kept lifting up their hands to heaven in prayer to the immortals for the happy return that all desired. One of them burst into tears and in her sorrow said to her neighbour: 'Poor Alcimede, tasting calamity at last, so late in life, with no hope now of an unclouded end! And what an evil stroke for Aeson too! Better for him if he had long since been lying in the grave, wrapped in his shroud, in happy ignorance of this ill-starred expedition. How I wish that the dark waves in which the lady Helle perished had closed over

Phrixus and his ram as well. Instead, the wicked monster actually spoke to him. Hence all this misery and heartache for Alcimede.' Such were the lamentations of the women at the Argonauts' departure.

In Jason's home, his many servants, men and women, had by now assembled. His mother too was there, clinging round his neck. The women were all overcome with grief; and his age-stricken father lying wrapped in bed, like a figure cut in stone, added his moans to theirs. But Jason soothed them in their sorrow with comfortable words, then, turning to his pages, told them to pick up his equipment; and they obeyed him in silence, with their eyes on the ground. But his mother held her son as fast as ever in her arms, weeping without restraint like a girl who in her loneliness falls into the arms of her old nurse, her one remaining friend, to ease her heart, fresh from the blows and insults of the stepmother who makes her life a misery. She weeps, and in such black despair that the sobs come welling up too fast for utterance. Thus Alcimede wept as she held her son in her arms, and in her anxious love she cried:

'Alas! I wish I could have died, forgetting all my cares, on the very day when I heard King Pelias make his evil proclamation, so that you, my child, might have buried me with your own dear hands. That was the only service I hoped you still might render me;

apart from that, you have long since repaid me for all a mother's care. But as it is, I that have stood as high as any woman in Achaea shall be left like a servant in an empty house, pining in misery for love of you, my pride and glory in days gone by, my first and last, my only son, seeing that the goddess has begrudged me the many children she bestows on others. How blind I was! Never once, not even in a dream, did I imagine that the flight of Phrixus could bring calamity to me.'

She wept and moaned, and the waiting-women round her joined in her lamentations. But Jason gently urged her to take heart.

'Mother,' he said, 'I beg you not to dwell so bitterly on your distress. No tears of yours will save me from misfortune; you will only be piling trouble upon trouble. We mortals cannot see what blows the gods may have in store for us; and you, for all your heartache, must endure your share with fortitude. Take courage from Athene's friendliness and the omens we have had from Heaven—the oracles of Phoebus could hardly have been more propitious. Remember too by what a noble company I am supported. Stay here, then, quietly in the house with your waiting-women, and do not be a bird of ill omen to my ship. I am going down to her now, together with my servants and retainers.'

With that he set out from the house, looking as he made his way through the crowd like Apollo when he issues from some fragrant shrine in holy Delos or Claros, or maybe at Pytho or in the broad realm of Lycia where Xanthus flows. The people, shouting as one man, saluted him; and Iphias, the aged priestess of Artemis, their city's Guardian, came forward and kissed his right hand, but was unable for all her eagerness to say a word to him as the crowd swept on. She was left there by the roadside, as the old are left by the young. Jason had passed and soon was out of sight.

When he had put the well-made city streets behind him, he came down to the beach of Pagasae, and his friends, awaiting him in a body by the ship, waved their hands in welcome. Jason paused before approaching, and they, who were all looking in his direction, were amazed to see Acastus and Argus speeding down from the city in defiance of the king's orders. Argus had thrown round his shoulders a black bull's hide which reached his feet, while Acastus wore a fine double cloak, a present from his sister Pelopeia. Jason refrained from asking them the many questions that occurred to him, and told the whole company to take their places for a conference. They all sat down in rows on the furled sail and the mast, which was lying there; and Aeson's son addressed them in a friendly spirit.

'*Argo,*' he said, 'has been fitted out as a ship should be. All is in order and ready for the voyage. So far as that is concerned, we could start at once, given only a favourable wind: But there is still one thing for you to do, my friends. We are all partners in this voyage to Colchis; partners too in the return to Hellas that we hope for. So now it is for you to choose the best man here to be our leader. And choose him in no partial spirit. Everything will rest with him. When we meet foreigners, it will be he who must decide whether to deal with them as enemies or friends.'

As he finished, the young men's eyes sought out the dauntless Heracles where he sat in the centre, and with one voice they called on him to take command. But he, without moving from his seat, raised his right hand and said: 'You must not offer me this honour. I will not accept it for myself, nor will I let another man stand up. The one who assembled this force must be its leader too.'

The magnanimity that Heracles had shown won their applause and they accepted his decision. Warlike Jason was delighted. He rose to his feet and addressed his eager friends.

'If you do indeed entrust me with this honourable charge, let nothing further keep us back—there have been enough delays already. The time has come for us to offer a pleasing sacrifice to Phoebus; we will prepare the feast at once. But while we are waiting for my overseers, who have been told to pick out some oxen from the herd and drive them here, let us drag the ship down into the water. Then you must get all the tackle on board and cast lots for your places on the rowing-benches. Also, we must build an altar on the beach for Apollo, the god of embarkation, who promised me through his oracles that he would be my counsellor and guide in our sea-faring if I offered him a sacrifice as I set forth on my mission for the king.'

He was the first to turn to the business in hand. The rest leapt to their feet and followed his example, piling their clothes on a smooth ledge of rock which in the past had been scoured by winter seas but now stood high and dry. First of all, at a word from Argus, they strengthened the ship by girding her with stout rope, which they drew taut on either side, so that her planks should not spring from their bolts but stand any pounding that the seas might give them. Next they quickly hollowed out a runway wide enough to take her beam, extending it into the sea as far as the prow would reach when they launched her, and as the trench advanced, digging deeper and deeper below the level of her stem. Then they laid smooth rollers on the bottom. This done, they tipped her down on to the first rollers, on top of which she was to glide along. Next, high up on both sides of the ship, they swung the oars inboard and fastened each handle to its tholepin so that a foot and a half projected. They themselves took their stance on either side, one behind the other, breasting the oars and pressing with their hands. And now Tiphys leapt on board to tell the young men when to push. He gave the order with a mighty shout and they put their backs into it at once. At the first heave they shifted her from where she lay; then strained forward with their feet to keep her on the move. And move she did. Between the two files of hustling, shouting men, Pelian *Argo* ran swiftly down. The rollers, chafed by the sturdy keel, groaned and reacted to the weight by putting up a pall of smoke. Thus she slid into the sea, and would have run still farther, had they not stood by and checked her with hawsers.

They fitted the oars to the tholes, and got the mast, the well-made sail, and the stores on board. Then, after satisfying themselves that all was shipshape, they cast lots for the benches, which held two oarsmen each. But the midships seat they gave to Heracles, selecting as his mate Ancaeus, the man from Tegea, and leaving this bench to the pair for their sole use, with no formalities and no recourse to chance. Also they all agreed that Tiphys should be the helmsman of their gallant ship.

Next, piling up shingle on the beach, they made a seaside altar for Apollo as god of shores and embarkation, and on the top they quickly laid down some dry logs of olive-wood. Meanwhile Jason's herdsmen had arrived, driving before them two oxen from their herd. The younger members of the party dragged the animals to the altar, the others came forward with the lustral water and barley-corns, and Jason, calling on Apollo, the god of his fathers, prayed in these words:

'Hear me, Lord, you that dwell in Pagasae and the city of Aesonis, which bears my father's name; you that promised me, when I sought an oracle in Pytho, to be my guide throughout my journey to its goal. You were the cause of my adventure: I look to you to bring my ship to Colchis and back to Hellas with my comrades safe and sound. Then we will once more glorify your altar, with a bull for each man that gets safely home; and I will bring you countless other gifts, some in Pytho, some in Ortygia. Come them, Archer-King, and accept the sacrifice we lay before you by way of payment for our passage on this ship—the very first that we have made for *Argo*. Lord, may your good will bring me luck as I cast off her cable; and may there be fair weather and a gentle breeze to carry us across the sea.'

As he prayed he sprinkled the barley-corns. And now Heracles and the powerful Ancaeus girt themselves for their task with the oxen. Heracles struck one of them full on the forehead with his club, and the steer, collapsing where it stood, sank to the ground. Ancaeus, with a bronze axe, smote the other on the nape of the neck, severing the mighty sinews, and it pitched forward on to both its horns. Their comrades promptly slit the animals' throats, then flayed them, chopped them up, and carved the flesh. They cut out the sacred pieces from the thighs, heaped them together, and after wrapping them in fat burnt them on faggots. Jason poured out libations of unmixed wine; and Idmon, watching intently, was glad to see bright flames all round the offering, and the smoke going up from them in dark spirals, exactly as it should. He spoke at once, telling them all that Apollo had in mind.

'For you,' he said, 'it is decreed by Heaven and Destiny that you should return to this place, bringing the fleece, though countless trials await you on the voyage out and back. I, on the other hand, am doomed by a god's malignant will to die in some remote spot on the Asian continent. From evil omens I have long since learnt my fate. Nevertheless, I left my country to embark, so that at home they might think well of me as one who sailed in *Argo*.'

This was all. The young men listening to the prophecy rejoiced to know that they would see their homes again, but were filled with grief for Idmon and his doom.

The time of day had come when the sun, after his midday rest, begins to throw the shadows of the rocks across the fields as he declines towards the evening dusk. So now they strewed the sand with a thick covering of leaves and lay down in rows above the grey line of the surf. They had beside them plentiful supplies of appetizing food and mellow wine which the stewards had drawn off in jugs; and presently they began to tell each other stories, as young men often do at a banquet to amuse themselves, when all goes pleasantly and nobody is in a mood to pick an ugly quarrel. But Jason, his resolution failing, retired within himself to brood on all his troubles. He looked like a man in despair, and Idas, noticing this, took him to task in a loud voice.

'Jason!' he cried. 'What are these deep thoughts that you are keeping to yourself? Tell us all what is the matter with you. Has panic got you in its grip? It often leaves a coward dumb. Then hear me swear. By my keen spear, with which I win the foremost honours in the wars, the spear that helps me more than Zeus himself, I swear that no disaster shall be fatal, no venture fail, with Idas at your back, even if a god comes up against us. That is the kind of ally you have got in me, the man from Arene.'

As he finished, he lifted a full beaker with both hands and drank the sweet unwatered wine till his lips and his dark beard were drenched with it. There was an outcry from them all; but it was Idmon who stood up and spoke his mind.

'Sir!' he said. 'Your words are deadly, and you will be the first to suffer for them. You are a bold man; but it seems that this strong wine has made you overbold, blinding your judgement when it led you to insult the gods. Surely there are other ways of putting fresh heart into a friend. Your whole effusion was outrageous. Have you not heard that long ago Aloeus' sons blasphemed, as you have done, against the happy gods? Those two were by no means your inferiors in courage; yet for all their prowess they were struck down by the swift arrows of Leto's Son.'

This brought a loud laugh from Aphareian Idas. Then, with an evil look at Idmon, he made an insolent reply:

'Come now, employ your second sight and tell me whether I too shall be brought by the gods to some such end as your Father provided for Aloeus' sons. Ask yourself too how you are going to get away from me alive, should you be caught out in an idle prophecy.'

He spoke in anger with the will to wound; and the quarrel would have gone still further, had not their comrades checked the contending pair with loud remonstrances. Jason himself intervened. And so did Orpheus. Raising his lyre in his left hand, he leapt to his feet and began a song.

He sang of that past age when earth and sky and sea were knit together in a single mould; how they were sundered after deadly strife; how the stars, the moon, and the travelling sun keep faithfully to their stations in the heavens; how mountains rose, and how, together with their Nymphs, the murmuring streams and all four-legged creatures came to be. How, in the beginning, Ophion and Eurynome, daughter of Ocean, governed the world from snow-clad Olympus; how they were forcibly supplanted, Ophion by Cronos, Eurynome by Rhea; of their fall into the waters of Ocean; and how their successors ruled the happy Titan gods when Zeus in his Dictaean cave was still a child, with childish thoughts, before the earthborn Cyclopes had given him the bolt, the thunder and lightning that form his glorious armament today.

The song was finished. His lyre and his celestial voice had ceased together. Yet even so there was no change in the company; the heads of all were still bent forward, their ears intent on the enchanting melody. Such was his charm—the music lingered in their hearts. But presently they mixed the libations that pious ritual prescribes for Zeus, poured them out on the burning tongues, and then in the dark betook themselves to sleep.

When radiant Dawn with her bright eyes beheld the towering crags of Pelion, and the headlands washed by wind-driven seas stood sharp and clear, Tiphys awoke and quickly roused his comrades to embark and fix the oars. At the same moment there came an awe-inspiring call from the harbour of Pagasae; and Pelian *Argo* herself, who was chafing to be off, cried out, for she carried a sacred beam from the Dodonian oak which Athene had fitted in the middle of her stem. So they followed one another to the rowing-benches and, taking their allotted places, sat down in proper order with their equipment by them. Ancaeus sat amidships beside the mighty bulk of Heracles, who laid his club near by and made the ship's keel underfoot sink deep into the water. And now the hawsers were hauled in and they poured libations on the sea.

Jason wept as he turned his eyes away from the land of his birth. But the rest struck the rough sea with their oars in time with Orpheus' lyre, like young men bringing down their quick feet on the earth in unison with one another and the lyre, as they dance for Apollo round his altar at Pytho, or in Ortygia, or by the waters of Ismenus. Their blades were swallowed by the waves, and on either side the dark salt water broke into foam, seething angrily in answer to the strong men's strokes. The armour on the moving ship glittered in the sunshine like fire; and all the time she was followed by a long white wake which stood out like a path across a green plain.

All the gods looked down from heaven that day, observing *Argo* and the spirit shown by her heroic crew, the noblest seamen of their time; and from the mountain heights the Nymphs of Pelion admired Athene's work and the gallant Argonauts themselves, tugging at the oars. Cheiron son of Philyra came down from the high ground to the sea and wading out into the grey surf waved his great hand again and again and wished the travellers a happy home-coming. His wife came too. She was carrying Peleus' little boy Achilles on her arm, and she held him up for his dear father to see.

Till they had left the harbour and its curving shores behind them, the ship was in the expert hands of Tiphys, wise son of Hagnias, who used the polish steering-oar to keep her on her course. But now they stept the tall mast in its box and fixed it with forestays drawn taut on either bow; then hauled the sail up to the masthead and unfurled it. The shrill wind filled it out; and after making the halyards fast on deck, each round its wooden pin, they sailed on at their ease past the long Tisaean headland, while Orpheus played his lyre and sang them a sweet song of highborn Artemis, Saver of ships and Guardian of those peaks that here confront the sea, and of the land of Iolcus. Fish large and small came darting out over the salt sea depths and gambolled in their watery wake, led by the music like a great flock of sheep that have had their fill of grass and follow their shepherd home to the gay sound of some rustic melody from his high-piping reed. And the wind, freshening as the day wore on, carried *Argo* on her way.

Already dim, the rich Pelasgian land was quickly out of view; and pressing on they passed the rocky flanks of Pelion. Cape Sepias disappeared, and sea-girt Sciathus hove in sight. Then far away they saw Peiresiae and under a clear sky the mainland coastline of Magnesia and the tomb of Dolops. Here, as the wind had veered against them, they beached their ship at nightfall, and in the dark, while the sea ran high, they made a sacrifice of sheep in the hero's honour. For two days they lingered on this coast, but on the third they hoisted their broad canvas and put out to sea. The beach is still called *Argo*'s Aphetae because she took off there.

Forging ahead they ran past Meliboea, leaving its stormy beaches on their lee. And in the morning they saw Homole sloping down to the sea quite close to them. They skirted it, and had not long to wait before they passed the mouth of the River Amyrus, and presently could see Eurymenae and the scarred ravines of Ossa and Olympus. Then, running all night before the wind, they made Pallene, where the hills rise up from Cape Canastra. And as they sailed on in the dawn, Mount Athos rose before them, Athos in Thrace, the peak of which, though as far from Lemnos as a well-found merchantman can travel by evening, throws its shadow over the island right up to Myrine. For the Argonauts there was a stiff breeze all that day and through the night; *Argo*'s sail was stretched. But with the sun's first rays there came a calm, and it was by rowing that they reached the rugged isle of Lemnos, where once the Sintians lived.

Here, in the previous year, the women had run riot and slaughtered every male inhabitant. The married men, seized with loathing for their lawful wives, had cast them off, conceiving an unruly passion for the captured girls they brought across the sea from raids in Thrace. The Lemnian wives had for long neglected the homage due to Aphrodite, and this was the angry Cyprian's punishment. Unhappy women! Their soul-destroying and insensate jealousy drove them to kill not only their husbands and the girls who had usurped their beds, but every male as well in order that they might not have to pay the price one day for this atrocious massacre. The only woman to forbear was Hypsipyle. She spared her aged father Thaos, who was king of Lemnos, and sent him drifting over the sea inside a chest, in the hope that he might yet escape. And so he did. Some fishermen dragged him ashore at the island then called Oenoe, but later renamed Sicinus after the son whom the nymph Oenoe bore to Thoas.

The Lemnian women found it an easier thing to look after cattle, don a suit of bronze, and plough the earth for corn than to devote themselves, as they had done before, to the tasks of which Athene is the patroness.

Nevertheless they lived in dire dread of the Thracians; and they cast many a glance across the intervening sea in case they might be coming. So when they saw *Argo* rowing up to the island, they at once equipped themselves for war and poured out in wild haste from the gates of Myrine, like ravening Thyiads, thinking that the Thracians had come. Hypsipyle joined them, dressed in her father Thoas' armour. It was a panic-stricken rabble, speechless and impotent with fear, that streamed down to the beach.

Meanwhile the Argonauts despatched Aethalides from their ship. He was the swift herald to whom they entrusted their messages and the wand of his own father, Hermes, who had endowed him with an all-embracing memory that never failed. He has long since been lost in the inexorable waters of Acheron, yet even so, Lethe has not overwhelmed his soul, whose destiny it is to be for ever changing its home, now staying with the dead men down below, now with the living under the beams of the sun. But why should I enlarge on the story of Aethalides? What he did now was to persuade Hypsipyle, as the day was spent, to let the travellers stay there for the night. But even when morning came, bringing a breeze from the north, they did not cast their hawsers off.

The Lemnian women made their way through the town to take their seats in the meeting-place. Hypsipyle herself had summoned them, and when the great assembly was complete, she rose to give them her advice.

'My friends,' she said, 'we must conciliate these people by our generosity. Let us supply them with food, good wine, and all that they may want to have with them on board, so as to make sure that they shall never come inside our walls, or get to know us well, as they would do if they were driven by their needs to mingle with us freely. The evil news of what we did would travel everywhere. It was a great crime that we committed, and one by no means likely to endear us to these men, if they came to know it, or indeed to others. Well, you have heard what I propose. If any woman among you has a better plan, let her stand up. It was for that purpose that I brought you here.'

After Hypsipyle had finished and sat down on her father's marble throne, the next to rise was her dear nurse Polyxo, an aged woman tottering on withered feet and leaning on a staff, but none the less determined to be heard. Four young girls were sitting by her, their virginal appearance contrasting with Polyxo's crown of white hair. She made her way to the centre of the meeting-place, raised her bowed head with a painful effort and began:

'Hypsipyle is right. We must accommodate these strangers: it is better to give than to be robbed. But that alone will not ensure your future happiness. What if the Thracians attack us, or some other enemy appears? Such things happen. And they happen unannounced—you saw how these men came. But even if Heaven spares us that calamity, there are many troubles worse than war that you will have to meet as time goes on. When the older ones among us have died off, how are you younger women, without children, going to face the miseries of age? Will the oxen yoke themselves? Will they go out into the fields and drag the ploughshare through the stubborn fallow? Will they watch the changing seasons and reap at the right time? As for myself, though Death still shudders at the sight of me, I have the feeling that the coming years will see me in the grave, duly and solemnly buried before the bad times come. But I do advise you younger ones to think. Salvation lies before you at your very feet, if only you will entrust your homes, your livestock, and your splendid city to these visitors.'

Polyxo's speech was greeted with applause from every side. They liked her plan; and Hypsipyle immediately stood up again and said, 'Since you are all agreed, I will send a messenger to the ship at once.' And turning to Iphinoe, who was at her side, 'Go, Iphinoe, and ask the captain of this expedition, whoever he may be, to come to my house and hear what the people have decided—it will please him. And tell his men that they may land, if they wish to do so, without fear and come into our town as friends.' With that, she dismissed the meeting and set out for home.

Iphinoe meanwhile presented herself to the Minyae, and when they asked what had brought her, she poured out her tale: 'The lady Hypsipyle, daughter of Thaos, sent me here to invite the captain of your ship, whoever he may be, to come and hear from her what the people have decided—she said it would please him. Also I am to tell the rest of you that you may land at once, if you wish to do so, and come into the town as friends.'

This struck them all as a very fit and proper welcome. They thought that Thaos must be dead and Hypsipyle, his only daughter, queen. So they urged Jason to set out at once and themselves prepared to go.

Jason fastened round his shoulders a purple cloak of double width which Pallas Athene, the Lady of Trito, had made and given him when she was laying down the props for *Argo*'s keel and showing him how to measure timber for the cross-beams with a rule. The brilliance of this mantle outdid the rising sun. It was of crimson cloth surrounded by a purple border and embroidered at each end with a number of distinct and curious designs.

Here were the Cyclopes sitting at work on an imperishable thunderbolt for Zeus the King. One ray was lacking to complete its splendour, and this lay spurting flame as they beat it out with their iron hammers.

And here were shown Antiope's two sons, Amphion and Zethus, with the town of Thebes, as yet unfortified. They were busy laying its foundations. Zethus was shouldering a mountain peak—he seemed to find it heavy work. Amphion walked behind, singing to a golden lyre; and a boulder twice as large as that of Zethus came trundling after him.

Next, Aphrodite of the long locks, wielding Ares' formidable shield. On the left side her tunic had slipped down from her shoulder to her forearm. It hung below her breast, and all was mirrored to perfection in the bronze shield that she held in front of her.

Elsewhere a woodland pasturage was shown with oxen grazing. For these a battle was afoot. Electryon's sons had been attacked by a band of Taphian raiders, who wished to walk off with their cattle. The dewy grass was drenched with their blood. But the herdsmen were too few, and the larger force had got the upper hand.

Next came a race between two chariots. In the leading car was Pelops, shaking the reins, with Hippodameia beside him. And close behind came Oenomaus, with the Myrtilus driving the horses. Oenomaus was trying to catch Pelops with a spear-cast in the back.

But just as he had poised his spear, the axle of his chariot twisted and broke in the hub; and out he fell.

And here was Phoebus Apollo, pictured as a sturdy youth shooting an arrow at the gigantic Tityos, who was boldly dragging off his mother Leto by her veil. Tityos was the lady Elare's son; but he was nursed and borne again by Mother Earth.

Phrixus the Minyan was also shown together with his ram. So vividly were they portrayed, the ram speaking and Phrixus listening, that as you looked you would have kept quiet in the fond hope of hearing some wise words from their lips. And still you would have gazed and still have hoped.

Such was the cloak that Athene, Lady of Trito, had made for Jason. In his right hand he held another gift, a light spear that Atalanta had given him, when she welcomed him in Maenalus, in token of her friendship and her strong desire to join him in the quest. But he had dissuaded her, fearing the bitter quarrels that a lovely girl would cause.

Jason set out on his way to the city, looking like that bright star whose beautiful red beams, piercing the darkness as he rises over the roof-tops, delight a girl shut up in her new bridal-bower and longing for the youth for whom her parents destine her, still far away in foreign lands. Thus Jason looked as he approached the city, and no sooner was he through the gates than the women of the town came flocking after him, charmed by their visitor's appearance. But Jason kept his eyes on the ground and walked resolutely on till he reached Hypsipyle's royal palace. There the double doors with their closely fitted panels were thrown open for him by the maids; and Iphinoe led him quickly through the noble hall and brought him to a polished chair, in which he sat down facing her mistress.

Hypsipyle turned her eyes aside and blushed as maidens do. Yet for all her modesty, her speech was calculated to deceive.

'Stranger,' she said, 'why have you stayed so long outside our city—a city that has lost its men? They have migrated to the mainland to plough the fields of Thrace. But let me tell you the whole sorry tale; I wish you all to know the truth. When my father Thoas was king our men-folk used to sail across from here to the mainland opposite and raid the Thracian farmsteads from their ships. They brought home plenty of booty, and they brought women too. But that malignant goddess Aphrodite had for some time had her eye on them. And now she struck, depriving them of all sense of right and wrong. As a result they conceived a loathing for their wedded wives; they turned them out of doors; and then the brutes indulged their passion by sleeping with the captives of their spears. For a long time we put up with this. We hoped there might be a change of

33

heart before it was too late. But the evil grew; and it had a double consequence. In every household, the lawful children were neglected, while a bastard generation was growing up. Meanwhile unmarried girls, besides the mothers who had lost their homes, were left to wander in the streets. No father took the slightest notice of his daughter; for all he cared, a cruel stepmother could kill her in his sight. No son was ready now to protect his mother from outrage. No brother loved his sisters as he should. Whether at home or dining out, dancing or talking politics, the men could think of nothing but the captured girls. But at last some god inspired us with a desperate resolve. We had the courage, when the men returned one day from Thrace, to shut the city-gates against them, in the hope that they might come to their senses, or take themselves elsewhere, trollops and all. In the end they begged us for all the male children left in the town, and so went back to Thrace. And there they are now, making a living from its snowy fields.

'So I invite you all to stay here and settle with us. If you yourself accept and the prospect pleases you, my royal father's sceptre shall certainly be yours. And I have no fear that you may think poorly of our land. It has the richest soil of any isle in the Aegean Sea. But first go to your ship and tell your comrades what I say. And pray do not avoid the city any more.'

Thus she glossed over the massacre and what had really happened to the men.

'Hypsipyle,' Jason replied, 'we need your help, and all you may give us will indeed be welcome. I shall come back to the city when I have told my people everything. But I must leave this island and its sovereignty to you. I refuse, not through indifference, but because a hazardous adventure calls me on.'

As he finished, he touched her right hand; then quickly turned and went. Countless young girls ran up from every side and danced round him in their joy, till he had passed through the city-gates. Then, when he had reported to his friends all that Hypsipyle had summoned him to hear, the girls drove down to the beach in smooth-running wagons laden with gifts. And they did not find it difficult to make the Argonauts come home with them for entertainment. Cypris, the goddess of desire, had done her sweet work in their hearts. She wished to please Hephaestus, the great Artificer, and save his isle of Lemnos from ever lacking men again.

Jason himself set out for Hypsipyle's royal home, and the rest scattered as chance took them—all but Heracles, who chose to stay by the ship with a few select companions. Soon the whole city was alive with dance and banquet. The scent of burnt-offerings filled the air; and all of the immortals, it was Here's glorious son Hephaestus and Cypris herself whom their song

and sacrifices were designed to please. Day followed
day, and still they did not sail. Indeed there is no
knowing when they would have left if Heracles had
not summoned a meeting, from which the women were
excluded, and sharply admonished his friends.

'My good sirs,' he began, not without irony. 'Are we
exiled for manslaughter? Cast out for killing relatives
at home? Or have we come here for brides, not fan-
cying our own women there? Are we really content to
stay and cultivate the soil of Lemnos? We shall get no
credit, I assure you, by shutting ourselves up with a set
of foreign women all this time. And it is no good pray-
ing for a miracle. Fleeces do not come to people of
their own accord. We might as well go home, leaving
this captain of ours to spend all day in Hypsipyle's
arms till he has won the admiration of the world by
repopulating Lemnos.'

Such was the force of his rebuke that not a man
could look him in the eye or answer him. With no
more said, the meeting broke up and they hurried off
to make ready for departure. But when the women got
wind of their intention, they came running down and
swarmed round them, moaning for grief, as bees come
pouring out from their rocky hive when the meadows
are gay with dew, and buzz about the lilies, flitting to
and fro to take their sweet toll from the flowers. There
was a loving hand and a kind word for every man,

36

with many a prayer to the happy gods for his safe return. Hypsipyle took Jason's hands in hers and prayed in tears for the lover she was losing.

'Go,' she said, 'and may the gods bring you and all your comrades home with the golden fleece for the king, since that is what you have set your heart on. This island and my father's sceptre will be waiting for you if you ever choose to come again when you are back in Hellas. You could easily collect a host of emigrants from other towns. But that is not what you will wish; something tells me that it will not happen. Nevertheless, remember Hypsipyle when you are far away and when you are at home. But tell me what I am to do if the gods allow me to become a mother; and I will gladly do it.'

Jason was moved. 'Hypsipyle,' he said, 'may the happy gods grant all the prayers you made on my behalf. But I hope that you will not think ill of me if I elect, with Pelias' permission, to live in my own country. Release from toil is all I ask of Heaven. But if I am not destined to return to Hellas from my travels, and you bear me a son, send him when he is old enough to Pelasgian Iolcus. I should like him to console my father and mother in their grief if he finds them still alive, and to care for them at their own fireside at home with no interference from the king.'

With that, Jason led the way on board. The other

chieftains followed him, went to their seats and manned the oars; Argus loosed the stern-cable from its sea-beaten rock; and they struck the water lustily with their long blades of pine.

In the evening, at the suggestion of Orpheus, they beached the ship at Samothrace, the island of Electra daughter of Atlas. He wished them, by a holy initiation, to learn something of the secret rites, and so sail on with greater confidence across the formidable sea. Of the rites I say no more, pausing only to salute the isle itself and the Powers that dwell in it, to whom belong the mysteries of which we must not sing.

From Samothrace they rowed on eagerly over the deep gulf of Melas, with the land of the Thracians on the left, and Imbros northward on the right. And just as the sun was setting they reached the foreland of the Chersonese. There they met a strong wind from the south, set their sail to it and entered the swift current of the Hellespont, which takes its name from Athamas's daughter. By dawn they had left the northern sea; by nightfall they were coasting the Rhoetean shore, inside the straits, with the land of Ida on their right. Leaving Dardania behind, they set course for Abydos, and after that they passed in turn Percote, Abarnis with its sandy beach, and sacred Pityeia. Before dawn, *Argo* by dint of sail and oar was through the darkly swirling Hellespont.

In the Propontis there is an island sloping steeply to the sea, close to the rich mainland of Phrygia, and parted from it only by a low isthmus barely raised above the waves. The isthmus, with its two shores, lies east of the River Aesepus; and the place itself is called Bear Mountain by the people round about. It is inhabited by a fierce and lawless tribe of aborigines, who present an astounding spectacle to their neighbours. Each of these earthborn monsters is equipped with six great arms, two springing from his shoulders, and four below from his prodigious flanks. But the isthmus and the plain belonged to the Doliones, who had for king the noble Cyzicus, son of Aeneus and Aenete, daughter of the godlike Eusorus. These people were never troubled by the fearsome aborigines: Poseidon, from whom they were descended, saw to that.

Argo, pressing on with a stiff breeze from Thrace behind her, reached this coast and ran into a harbour called Fairhaven. Here, on the advice of Tiphys, they discarded their small anchor-stone and left it at the spring of Artacie, replacing it with a heavier and more suitable rock. Later, at the prompting of Apollo, the original stone was transferred by the Ionian followers of Neleus to the temple of Jasonian Athene, where it was rightly treated as a sacred relic.

The Doliones and Cyzicus their king received the Argonauts in a friendly spirit, and when told who they were and the object of the expedition, offered them hospitality, inviting them to row farther in and moor in the town harbour. Here they built an altar on the beach for Apollo, god of happy landings, and made him a sacrifice. The king himself supplied them with the good wine they lacked and also with sheep—he had been warned by an oracle that when some such dedicated band of noblemen arrived he must receive them with civility and no display of arms. This man, with the soft down on his cheeks, somewhat resembled Jason. He too had no children to delight him in his home, where his wife, the gentle lady Cleite, daughter of Percosian Merops, had not as yet experienced the pangs of childbirth. Indeed he had but lately brought her from the mainland opposite, paying a princely dowry to her father. Nevertheless he left his young wife in their bridal chamber and joined his visitors at dinner with no misgivings. And they questioned one another. Cyzicus asked about their destination and the task that Pelias had set them; and in answer to their own inquiries he told them about the neighbouring towns and the whole broad Propontic Gulf. But farther than that his knowledge did not go, much as they wished to learn what lay beyond.

In the morning some of the Argonauts climbed towards the top of Dindymum in the hope of seeing for themselves the waters they would have to cross—the way they took is still called Jason's path. Another party brought the ship from her former anchorage to the harbour of Chytus.

But now the earthborn savages, coming from the other side, dashed down the mountain and blocked the mouth of the ample harbour of Chytus with boulders, in an attempt to pen them like wild beasts in a trap. However, Heracles had been left there with the younger men. He quickly bent his recurved bow and brought a number of the monsters down. The rest retaliated by pelting him with jagged rocks. And I cannot but surmise that these redoubtable beasts were bred by Here, Wife of Zeus, as an extra labour for Heracles. But just at this moment, the rest of the Argonauts, who had turned back before reaching the summit, appeared on the scene to take their part in the slaughter. The monsters charged with fury more than once, but the young warriors were ready for them with their spears and arrows and in the end they killed them all.

When the long timbers for a ship have been hewn by the woodman's axe they are laid in rows on a beach and there they lie and soak till they are ready to receive the bolts. That is how these fallen monsters looked, stretched out in a row on the grey beach by the harbour mouth. Some were sprawling in a mass with their limbs on shore and their heads and breasts in the sea. Some lay the other way about; their heads were resting on the sands and their feet were deep in the water. But in either case they were carrion for birds and fish. The day was won and the Argonauts had no more to fear.

They loosed the hawsers of their ship, caught the breeze, and forged ahead through a choppy sea. They sailed all day, but the wind began to fail at dusk. Then it veered against them, freshened to a gale, and sent them scudding back towards their hospitable friends the Doliones. And that same night they went ashore. The rock round which they cast the ship's hawsers in their haste is still called the Sacred Rock.

But no one had the sense to note that they were landing on the very island they had left; and in the darkness the Doliones themselves failed to realize that the Argonauts were back. They thought that some Pelasgian raiders had landed, Macrians perhaps. So they donned their armour and attacked. And now there was a clash of shields and ashen spears as the two parties met, with the impact of a forest fire when it pounces on dry brushwood and leaps into the sky. The Doliones were plunged into all the horrors and turmoil of a war.

Their king himself was not allowed to cheat the Fates and come home from the battle to his young wife in her bridal bed. Jason, as the king swung round to face him, leapt in and struck him full in the breast, shattering the bone with his spear. Cyzicus sank down on the sands; he had had his span of life, and more than that no mortal can command—we are like birds trapped in the wide net of Destiny. And so this man was caught: he thought he had escaped the worst that the Argonauts might do to him, but that very night he fought them and died. And he was not their only champion to fall. Heracles killed Telecles and Megabrontes; Acastus killed Sphodris; Zelys and stalwart Gephyrus fell to Peleus. Telamon with his great ashen spear killed Basileus; Idas killed Promeus; and Clytius, Hyacinthus; while Castor and Polydeuces despatched Megalossaces and Phlogius. Meleager added two to these, the dauntless Itymoneus, and Artaces, a dashing leader. Their countrymen still honour all the slain as heroes.

The rest gave way and fled in panic, like a flock of doves with a swift hawk after them. There was a wild rush for the gates, and the city was soon loud with lamentation for the catastrophe. Then came the dawn and taught both sides their grievous and irreparable error. The Minyae were overcome with sorrow when they saw Cyzicus lying in the dust and blood; and for three whole days they and the Doliones wailed for him and tore their hair. Then they marched three times round the dead king in their bronze equipment, laid him in his tomb, and held the customary games out on the grassy plain, where the barrow they raised for him can still be seen by people of a later age.

Cleite the king's bride was unable to face life alone, with her husband in the grave. Capping the evil she had suffered with a worse one of her own devising, she took a rope and hanged herself by the neck. Her death was bewailed even by the woodland nymphs, who caused the many tears they shed to unite in a spring, which the people call Cleite in memory of a peerless but unhappy bride. It was a day of horror for the Doliones, the worst that Zeus had ever sent their women or their men. Not one of them could even bear to eat, and such was their grief that for a long time they let their hand-mills stand idle and lived on uncooked food. To this very day the Ionians of Cyzicus, when they make their yearly libations, grind the meal for the cakes at the public mill.

For twelve days after this there was foul weather day and night, and the Argonauts were unable to put out. But towards the end of the next night, while Acastus and Mopsus watched over their comrades, who had long been fast asleep, a halcyon hovered over the golden head of Aeson's son and in its piping voice announced the end of the gales. Mopsus heard it and understood the happy omen. So when the sea-bird, still directed by a god, flew off and perched on the mascot of the ship, he went to Jason, who lay comfortably wrapped in fleeces, woke him quickly with a touch and said:

'My lord, you must climb this holy peak to propitiate Rhea, Mother of all the happy gods, whose lovely throne is Dindymum itself—and then the gales will cease. I learnt this from a halcyon just now: the sea-bird flew above you as you slept and told me all. Rhea's dominion covers the winds, the sea, the whole earth, and the gods' home on snow-capped Olympus. Zeus himself, the Son of Cronos, gives place to her when she leaves her mountain haunts and rises into the broad sky. So too do the other blessed ones; all pay the same deference to that dread goddess.'

This was welcome news to Jason, who leapt up from his bed rejoicing. He hastily woke the rest and told them how Mopsus had interpreted the signs. They set to work at once. The younger men took some oxen from the stalls and began to drive them up the steep path to the top of Dindymum. The others loosed the hawsers from the sacred rock and rowed *Argo* to the Thracian anchorage. Then, leaving a few of their comrades in the ship, they too climbed the mountain. From the summit they could see the Macrian heights and the whole length of the opposite Thracian coast—it almost seemed that they could touch it. And far away on the one side they saw the misty entrance to the Bosporus and the Mysian hills, and on the other the flowing waters of Aesepus and the city and Nepeïan plain of Adresteia.

Standing in the woods, there was an ancient vine with a massive trunk withered to the roots. They cut this down to make a sacred image of the mountain goddess; and when Argus had skilfully shaped it, they set it up on a rocky eminence under the shelter of some tall oaks, the highest trees that grow, and made an altar of small stones near by. Then, crowned with oak-leaves, they began the sacrificial rites, invoking the Dindymian Mother, most worshipful, who dwells in Phrygia; and with her, Titias and Cyllenus. For these two are singled out as dispensers of doom and assessors to the Idaean Mother from the many Idaean Dactyls of Crete. They were borne in the Dictaean cave by the Nymph Anchiale as she clutched the earth of Oaxus with both her hands.

Jason, pouring libations on the blazing sacrifice, earnestly besought the goddess to send the stormy winds elsewhere. At the same time, by command of Orpheus, the young men in full armour moved round in a high-stepping dance, beating their shields with their swords to drown the ill-omened cries that came up from the city, where the people were still wailing for their king. This is why the Phrygians to this day propitiate Rhea with the tambourine and drum.

The goddess they invoked must have observed the flawless sacrifice with pleasure, for her own appropriate signs appeared. The trees shed abundant fruit; the earth at their feet adorned itself with tender grass; beasts left their lairs and thickets and came to them with wagging tails. And these were not her only miracles. Until that day there had been no running water on Dindymum. But now, with no digging on their part, a stream gushed out for them from the thirsty peak. And it did not cease to flow; the natives of the place still drink from it. They call it Jason's Spring.

As a finish to the rites, they held a feast on Bear Mountain in honour of Rhea and sang the praises of the venerable goddess. By dawn the wind had dropped and they rowed off from the island in a spirit of rivalry, each trying to outlast the others at the oars. The windless air had smoothed the waves on every side and put the sea to sleep. So they took advantage of the calm to drive the ship forward by their own power; and as she sped through the salt water, not even Poseidon's team, the horses for the whirlwind feet, could have overtaken her. Later, however, when the sea was roughened by the strong winds that blow down rivers in the afternoon, they wearied and relaxed. It was left to Heracles to bring the whole exhausted crew along with him, pulling his hardest with his great arms and sending shudders through the framework of the ship. They were anxious to reach the Mysian coast. But as they passed within sight of the mouth of the Rhyndacus and the great barrow of Aegaeon, not far from Phrygia,

Heracles, ploughing furrows in the choppy sea, broke his oar in half and fell sideways off the bench with one end in his hands while the other was swept away by the receding waves. He sat up, speechless and glaring. He was not used to idle hands.

They made their landfall at the time of day when the vine-dresser or ploughman, filled with thoughts of supper, reaches home at last and, pausing at the door, begrimed with dust, bends a weary knee and looks at his worn hands with a curse for the belly that commands such toil. They had struck the Cianian coast near Mount Arganthon and the estuary of Cius. And coming as they did with no hostile intent, they were kindly received by the Mysian inhabitants, who supplied their needs with sheep and wine in plenty. Some of the Argonauts went to fetch dry wood; some collected leaves from the fields and brought them in for bedding; others twirled firesticks; and others again mixed wine in the bowls for the feast that was to follow a sacrifice at nightfall to Apollo, god of happy landings.

But Heracles son of Zeus, leaving his friends to prepare the banquet, set out for the woods, anxious before all else to make himself a handy oar. Wandering about he found a pine that was not burdened with many branches nor had reached its full stature, but was like a slender young poplar in height and girth. He promptly laid his bow and quiver down, took off his lion-skin and began by loosening the pine's hold in the ground with blows of his bronze-studded club. Then he trusted to his own strength. With his legs wide apart and one broad shoulder pressed against the tree, he seized it low down with both hands and gripping hard he tore it out. Deep-rooted though it was, it came up clods and all like a ship's mast torn from its stays, together with the wedges, by a sudden squall in the stormy days when Orion sets in anger. Thus Heracles tore out the pine; then he picked it up, with his bow and arrows, lion-skin and club, and started to go back.

Meanwhile Hylas had gone off by himself with a bronze ewer in search of some hallowed spring where he could draw water for the evening meal and be in time to get everything ready, like a good servant, for his master's return. Heracles himself had trained him in these ways ever since he had taken him as a child from the house of his royal father, Theiodamas, whom he had ruthlessly killed at the head of his Dryopians after a quarrel about a ploughing ox. The doomed man was ploughing up a piece of fallow when Heracles, anxious to find a pretext for attacking the Dryopians, a lawless tribe, asked him for the ox and was refused. But the whole tale would take me too far from my present theme.

Hylas soon found a spring, which the people of the neighbourhood call Pegae. He reached it when the nymphs were about to hold their dances—it was the custom of all those who haunt that beautiful headland to sing the praise of Artemis by night. The nymphs of the mountain peaks and caverns were all posted some way off to patrol the woods; but one, the naiad of the spring, was just emerging from the limpid water as Hylas drew near. And there, with the full moon shining on him from a clear sky, she saw him in all his radiant beauty and alluring grace. Her heart was flooded by desire; she had a struggle to regain her scattered wits. But Hylas now leant over to one side to dip his ewer in; and as soon as the water was gurgling loudly round the ringing bronze she threw her left arm round his neck in her eagerness to kiss his gentle lips. Then with her right hand she drew his elbow down and plunged him in midstream.

The lord Polyphemus son of Eilatus, who had gone some way along the path in the hope of meeting the gigantic Heracles, was the only member of the company to hear the boy's cry. Led by the sound he rushed off towards Pegae, like a wild animal who hears the bleating of a distant flock and in his hunger dashes after them, only to find that the shepherds have forestalled him, the sheep are in the pen, and he is left to roar in protest till he tires. Thus Polyphemus groaned in his distress and shouted as he prowled about the place. But there was no answering voice. So he drew his great sword and began to extend the search, fearing that Hylas might have fallen to a wild beast or been ambushed by some men, who would have found the lonely boy an easy prey. Then, as he ran along the path brandishing his naked sword, he met Heracles himself hastening back to the ship through the darkness. Polyphemus knew him at once and blurted out his lamentable tale, gasping for breath:

'My lord! It falls to me to give you dreadful news. Hylas went out for water. He has not come back. Some brigands must have got him. Or beasts are tearing him to pieces. I heard him cry.'

When Heracles heard this, the sweat poured from his forehead and the dark blood boiled within him. In his fury he threw down the pine and rushed off, little caring where his feet were carrying him. Picture a bull stampeded from the water-meadows by a gadfly's sting. He takes to his heels. The herd and herdsmen are nothing to him now; and off he goes, sometimes pressing on without a stop, sometimes pausing to lift his mighty neck and bellow in his pain. Thus Heracles in his frenzy ran at top speed for a while without a break, then paused in his exertions to fill the distance with a ringing cry.

But now the morning star rose above the topmost peaks, and with it came a breeze. Tiphys urged his comrades to embark at once and take advantage of the wind. They went on board in eager haste, pulled up the anchor-stones and hauled the ropes astern. Struck full by the wind, the sail bellied out, and soon they rejoiced to find themselves far out at sea, passing Poseidon's Cape.

But presently, at the hour when bright-eyed Dawn comes up to light the eastern sky, and all the paths stand out and the fields glisten with dew, they realized that they had heedlessly left two of their numbers behind. Tumult and fierce recriminations followed: they had sailed without the bravest Argonaut of all. But Jason, paralysed by a sense of utter helplessness, added no words to either side in this dispute. He sat and ate his heart out, crushed by the calamity.

Telamon was enraged. 'You may well sit there at your ease,' he cried, 'since nothing suits you better than to abandon Heracles. You planned the whole affair yourself so that his fame in Hellas should not eclipse your own, if we have the good fortune to return. But why waste my breath? I am determined to go back, and that without consulting those friends of yours who abetted you in this plot.'

As he finished he made a rush at Tiphys, his eyes ablaze with angry fire. And they would soon have been on their way back to Mysia, forcing *Argo* through the sea against a stiff and steady breeze, if the two sons of the North Wind, Zetes and Calaïs, had not checked

Telamon with a stinging rebuke. Unhappy pair! A dreadful punishment was coming to them at the hands of Heracles for having thus cut short the search for him. He killed them in sea-girt Tenos on their way home from the games at Pelias' funeral, made a barrow over them and on top set a couple of pillars, one of which amazes all beholders by swaying to the breath of the roaring North Wind. But all this was yet to come. Now, they suddenly saw Glaucus, the sage spokesman of the sea-god Nereus, emerge from the salt depths. Raising his shaggy head and front, as far down as the waist, he laid his sturdy hand on the side of the ship and cried to the contending Argonauts:

'Why do you propose, in defiance of almighty Zeus, to bring the dauntless Heracles to Colchis? Argos is his place. There he is fated to serve his cruel master, Eurystheus; to accomplish twelve tasks; and if he succeeds in the few that yet remain, to join the immortals in their home. So let there be no regrets for him. Nor for Polyphemus, who is destined to found a famous city among the Mysians where Cius flows into the sea, and to meet his end in the broad land of the Chalybes. As for Hylas, who caused these two to go astray and so be left behind, a Nymph has lost her heart to him and made him her husband.'

With that, he plunged and was swallowed by the restless waves. The dark water swirled round him, broke into foam, and dashed against the hollow ship as she moved on.

The Argonauts were filled with joy, and Telamon went straight up to Jason. He gripped his hand, kissed him, and said, 'My lord, do not be angry with me if in a foolish moment I was blinded. An intolerable affront was forced from me in my distress. May the winds blow away the offence, and let us two, who always have been friends, be friends again.'

The son of Aeson answered him with wise forbearance. 'My good sir,' he said, 'you did indeed insult me grievously when you accused me, before all these, of having wronged a loyal friend. I was cut to the quick, but I am not going to nurse a grudge. For you were not quarrelling with me about a flock of sheep or worldly goods, but about a man, a comrade of your own. And I like to think that if the occasion arose you would stand up for me against others as boldly as you did for him.'

This was enough. They both sat down, united as they had been before, and Zeus concerned himself with the other pair. He destined Polyphemus to build in Mysia a city which should bear the river's name, and Heracles to resume his labours for Eurystheus. But before he left Mysia, Heracles threatened to lay waste the land if the people failed to find out for him what had become of Hylas, living or dead. The Mysians then gave him some of their best young men as hostages and solemnly swore that they would never abandon the search. For which reason the people of Cius enquire after Hylas son of Theiodamas to this very day, and take a friendly interest in the well-built city of Trachis, where Heracles settled the youthful hostages they had let him take from Cius.

All that day and through the following night a stiff breeze carried *Argo* on; but at daybreak there was not a breath of air. However, they saw land ahead. There was a beach that showed up from a bay, and it seemed to be a wide one. So they rowed the ship towards it and ran her ashore as the sun rose.

PENGUIN 60s CLASSICS

PENGUIN 60s CLASSICS

READ MORE IN PENGUIN

For complete information about books available from Penguin and how to order them, please write to us at the appropriate address below. Please note that for copyright reasons the selection of books varies from country to country.

IN THE UNITED KINGDOM: Please write to *Dept. EP, Penguin Books Ltd, Bath Road, Harmondsworth, Middlesex UB7 0DA.*

IN THE UNITED STATES: Please write to *Consumer Sales, Penguin USA, P.O. Box 999, Dept. 17109, Bergenfield, New Jersey 07621-0120.* VISA and MasterCard holders call 1-800-253-6476 to order Penguin titles.

IN CANADA: Please write to *Penguin Books Canada Ltd, 10 Alcorn Avenue, Suite 300, Toronto, Ontario M4V 3B2.*

IN AUSTRALIA: Please write to *Penguin Books Australia Ltd, P.O. Box 257, Ringwood, Victoria 3134.*

IN NEW ZEALAND: Please write to *Penguin Books (NZ) Ltd, Private Bag 102902, North Shore Mail Centre, Auckland 10.*

IN INDIA: Please write to *Penguin Books India Pvt Ltd, 706 Eros Apartments, 56 Nehru Place, New Delhi 110 019.*

IN THE NETHERLANDS: Please write to *Penguin Books Netherlands bv, Postbus 3507, NL-1001 AH Amsterdam.*

IN GERMANY: Please write to *Penguin Books Deutschland GmbH, Metzlerstrasse 26, 60594 Frankfurt am Main.*

IN SPAIN: Please write to *Penguin Books S. A., Bravo Murillo 19, 1° B, 28015 Madrid.*

IN ITALY: Please write to *Penguin Italia s.r.l., Via Felice Casati 20, I-20124 Milano.*

IN FRANCE: Please write to *Penguin France S. A., 17 rue Lejeune, F-31000 Toulouse.*

IN JAPAN: Please write to *Penguin Books Japan, Ishikiribashi Building, 2-5-4, Suido, Bunkyo-ku, Tokyo 112.*

IN GREECE: Please write to *Penguin Hellas Ltd, Dimocritou 3, GR-106 71 Athens.*

IN SOUTH AFRICA: Please write to *Longman Penguin Southern Africa (Pty) Ltd, Private Bag X08, Bertsham 2013.*